BOOK OF TOP TEN LISTS

By Holly Kowitt

Based on *Ned's Declassified School Survival Guide*
created by Scott Fellows

SCHOLASTIC INC.

New York   Toronto   London   Auckland   Sydney

Mexico City   New Delhi   Hong Kong   Buenos Aires

If you purchased this book without a cover, you should be
aware that this book is stolen property. It was reported
as "unsold and destroyed" to the publisher, and neither
the author nor the publisher has received any
payment for this "stripped book."

No part of this publication may be reproduced in whole or
in part, stored in a retrieval system, or transmitted in any
form or by any means, electronic, mechanical, photocopying,
recording, or otherwise, without written permission
of the publisher. For information regarding permission,
write to Scholastic Inc., Attention: Permissions
Department, 557 Broadway, New York, NY 10012.

ISBN 0-439-83161-X

© 2006 Viacom International Inc. All Rights Reserved.
Nickelodeon, Ned's Declassified School Survival Guide, and all related titles,
logos, and characters are trademarks of Viacom International Inc.

Published by Scholastic Inc. All rights reserved.

SCHOLASTIC and associated logos are trademarks and/or
registered trademarks of Scholastic Inc.

12 11 10 9 8 7 6 5 4 3   7 8 9 10/0

Printed in the U.S.A.

First printing, June 2006

Hey—check this out.

I've put together my own declassified book of Top Ten Lists. It has all you'll need to survive evil teachers, lame classes, scary school lunches, crushes who don't know you're alive, female bullies, and other daily traumas. You'll sooooo thank me for No-Fail Homework Excuses and Signs You Won't Be Sitting at the Cafeteria Cool Table. On the other hand, feel free to ignore Mr. Gross's Grooming Tips and Billy Loomer's Etiquette Pointers.

I've also given you inside stuff like Gordy's To-Do List, Rejected Themes for the School Dance, Questions on the Huge Crew Application, Perks of Being the School Weasel, Worst Jokes Going Around James Polk Middle School, and Farting Words.

As if that isn't enough, I've also thrown in Top Ten Numbers on My (Fantasy) Speed Dial, Questions That Keep Me Up at Night, and more. Could this book *get* any better?

Enjoy, and remember: Never pick your nose past the knuckle. . . .

Ned

PROFILE: NED BIGBY

AKA: Chicken Boy, Crouching Weasel, Wedge Picker, Dead Bigby

UNWANTED NOMINATION: School class president

CAMPAIGN SLOGAN: "Vote Ned or You're Dead"

BEST MOMENT: Organized Talentpalooza, Kissed Suzie Crabgrass, Rode Bike with Mat Hoffman

BASKETBALL TRYOUT RESULTS: Came up a little short

DUBIOUS CLAIM: "That was a way-lucky kick. I could sooooo take you."

WORST LATENESS EXCUSE: "I was trapped in a locker."

NOT-SO-SECRET CRUSH: Suzie Crabgrass

DISTURBING QUOTE: "If I were a girl, I'd be *thrilled* if I liked me."

MOST EMBARRASSING MOMENT: Used the girl's bathroom—but it was so long ago

NED'S TOP TEN NO-FAIL HOMEWORK EXCUSES

 You're such a great teacher, I don't need to do homework.

 The weasel ate my homework— Billy Loomer ate the weasel.

 Okay, okay—the dog ate it. Seriously!

 I gave it to you. Don't tell me you lost it!!!

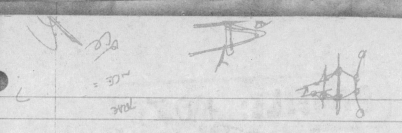

 5. Our house was burglarized, and they got away with my math book.

 6. Lisa Zemo sneezed on it.

 7. Timmy Toot Toot blasted it.

 8. My e-mail wasn't working, so I couldn't get the answers from Cookie.

 9. I threw it at someone who said you *weren't* the best teacher in school.

 10. It was due May first of *this* year? Dang!

PROFILE: MOZE

REAL NAME: Jennifer Mosely

EMBARRASSING MOMENT: Giant pimple registering 1.3 on the "zit-ker" scale

BIGGEST MISTAKE: Accidentally drilling hole in Mr. Chopsaw's hand

FAVORITE SUBJECT: Woodshop

TEACHER'S PRAISE: "The lathe is an instrument, and in your hands it's a Stradivarius."

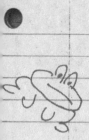

REAL NAME: Simon Nelson Cook

AKA: Wizard of Words, P. Cookie, Super Cookie, Cyber Dork, Cyborg

OCCUPATION: Middle school cyborg

REPUTATION: Half-man, half-machine

NEVER WITHOUT: Pocket computer attached to eyeglasses

FAVE ACTIVITY: Hacking into school server to change lunch menu

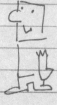

MOZE'S TOP TEN EXCUSES FOR THE WOLVES LOSING THE VOLLEYBALL CHAMPIONSHIP

 1. Scoop's flash got in my eye.

 2. The lunch lady predicted it—it was in the beans.

 3. Forgot our lucky underwear.

 4. The weasel let us down on defense.

 5. Hard to spike the ball over Suzie Crabgrass's ego.

 6. Ran out of volleyballs, had to use Life Science Baby.

7. One of our fans, Timmy Toot Toot, blew the game, if you know what I mean.

 8. Winning is for losers.

 9. We were distracted by Cookie in that cheerleading skirt.

 10. Mr. Gross cheered so much, his breath melted the net.

PROFILE: COOKIE

REAL NAME: Simon Nelson Cook

AKA: Wizard of Words, P. Cookie, Super Cookie, Cyber Dork, Cyborg

OCCUPATION: Middle school cyborg

REPUTATION: Half-man, half-machine

NEVER WITHOUT: Pocket computer attached to eyeglasses

FAVE ACTIVITY: Hacking into school server to change lunch menu

LOVE INTEREST: Vanessa

WIRED TO WEB: 24/7

LIKES: Computers, his friends, the ladies

DISLIKES: Ruining perfect attendance record, spelling bullies, out-of-the-way lockers

QUOTE: "Ever since I got a detention, my cool rating is through the roof!"

TOP TEN COOKIE INVENTIONS THAT DIDN'T GET PATENTED

1. Wedgie-repellent underwear with rip-away elastic band.

2. "Fart 'B' Gone"—an air-freshening helmet to wear near Tommy Toot Toot.

3. Cookie cutout (to avoid ruining perfect attendance record on sick days).

4. Hot new video game: "Escape from Sweeney's Class."

Geek tattoo engraver, featuring classic geek designs like "Skull with Glasses" screen saver and a flaming computer.

 Locker-phone with direct lines to Supermodel Martika and Bill Gates.

 Dodgeball-bot. Dirga-proof cyborg that takes gym class for you: does push-ups, runs, and gets picked last.

 Bully Loomer Advance Detection System: sensors register armpit farts within ten-foot radius.

 Cafeteria Table Cool-o-meter™. Measures level of coolness at your table, ranging from "Uncool" to "Seth Powers."

 The "substitute ray" turns any teacher into a substitute teacher.

PROFILE:
MR. DUSTY CHOPSAW

OCCUPATION: Shop teacher

FAKE BODY PART: Prosthetic hand

STUDENT PRAISE: "He's got more fingers than the last shop teacher."

APPEARANCE: Tall, splintery, dusty

PET PEEVE: Accidentally throwing hand into woodchipper, using saw to cut life science dolls in half

BEST CHRISTMAS GIFT: Two front teeth

PHILOSOPHY: "You gotta be strong like oak, pliable like bamboo."

MOST UNTRUE RUMOR: Whole body is made of wood

FIRST TRUE LOVE: His bandsaw

QUOTE: "She still cuts like the first day I laid eyes on her."

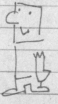

MOZE'S TOP TEN SECRET SURPRISES ABOUT CHOPSAW

 1. He sleeps on a bed of woodchips.

 2. His mother is half birch.

 3. As a child, he had friends over for lumber parties.

 4. What he wants on his gravestone: "He Came, He Saw, He Sanded."

 5. Has lifelong pencil-chewing problem.

 6. He lost finger in the Birdhouse of '92.

Spends nights watching "The Sawing Channel."

 Collects used toothpicks.

 Wears designer safety goggles on dates.

 He loves back-to-school chopping.

PROFILE: GORDY

OCCUPATION: School janitor

OBSESSION: Nabbing school weasel, avoiding work, and avoiding Vice Principal Crubbs

TOOLS: Sink, mop, bucket, jackhammer, ICBM missile, parachute, Weasel Chow, disco ball

ACTIVITIES: Burning items in Lost & Found, having "Gordy" time

PET PEEVES: Cleaning, working

EDUCATION: He's been to law school five times.

FREQUENT ANNOUNCEMENT: "Ned to the janitor's closet"

CODE NAME: WeaselOne

MORAL PRINCIPLE: "I can't give a pickax to an unsupervised minor."

WHAT HE GAVE HIM INSTEAD: A jackhammer

QUOTE: "I'll let the night guy get that."

GORDY'S TO-DO LIST

1. Get more Weasel Chow.

2. Burn rest of stuff in Lost & Found.

3. Sneak in quick nap before breakfast.

4. Buy air freshener for Frank-&-Beans Day.

5. Replace weasel nuggets on Can't Fail Trap #43.

6. Patent the "Human Hamster Ball."

 7. Finish reading *Weasel Psychology*.

 8. Buy more barf powder.

 9. Rig up "Cool Table Monitor" to help Ned get date with Suzie.

 10. Inspect clogged toilet. Leave for night guy.

PROFILE:
SUZIE CRABGRASS

OCCUPATION: Class overachiever

OBSESSION: Getting elected class president

HOME: Cafeteria "cool" table

PERSONALITY: Sweet smile, killer instinct

CHIEF RIVAL: Moze

EXTRACURRICULAR: Volleyball team co-captain and co-head cheerleader with Moze

HANDS OUT: Free beany-kitties

MOTIVE: To "out-fuzzy" the competition

BEST ELECTION GIVEAWAY: Candy bars saying "Ned Is a Total Loser"

QUOTE: "Ned, I'll officially apologize to you tomorrow after I win. Candy bar?"

TOP TEN REASONS WHY SUZIE SHOULD DATE NED

 1. He's cute and cuddly, like a beany-kitty.

 2. He's easy to flip in gym class.

 3. He became a hero when he freed Sweeney's class on Pizza Day.

 4. He's no longer known as "Wedge Picker."

 5. Where Ned goes, lightbulbs follow.

6. Because it would bother Moze—a lot!

 7. A whole new locker to decorate.

 8. Unlike Seth Powers, he won't wear a warm-up suit to the school dance.

 9. Already have "Ned Is a Total Loser" candy bars for when they break up.

 10. If you can't beat him, date him.

PROFILE: COCONUT HEAD

NICKNAME: Coconut Head

KNOWN FOR: The world's worst haircut

WHAT OTHERS CAN LEARN: Don't let your mom near scissors.

SECRET CRUSH: The Huge Crew

WOULD LIKE TO BE: Kissed

WILL SETTLE FOR: Getting beaten up

LIKES: Tough girls

BIGGEST FEAR: Billy Loomer

DREAM DATE: Seven minutes in Gordy's Closet with the Crew

QUOTE: "Aren't you gonna throw me? I'm cute and tossable!"

TOP TEN BEST THINGS ABOUT BEING COCONUT HEAD

 1. Would fit in at a Hawaiian luau.

 2. Your style is all your own—and no one else wants it!

 3. Don't have to worry about getting unflattering nickname.

 4. Save money on professional haircuts.

 5. Asking a gift shop if they have "Coconut Head" mini license plates.

6. Easy to spot in a swimming pool.

 7. Can feel superior to guys named "Pineapple Head."

 8. Two words: Huge Crew.

 9. Insisting people call you "Mr. Coconut Head."

 10. Doesn't matter if real name is embarrassing. No one remembers it anyway.

PROFILE: DIRGA

DESCRIPTION: Gym teacher

NICKNAME: Dirga

HABITAT: Rusty lockers filled with dirty tube socks

EDUCATION: State university on dodgeball scholarship

ADVICE FOR EVERY PROBLEM: "Put some arm into it!"

PET PEEVE: People who cross the free-throw line

FAVORITE COMMAND: "Just run until you puke."

INFLICTS: Daggers, herkies, handsprings, and tumble rolls

SKILLS: Whistle-twirling, basketball-inflating

QUOTE: "I don't care if your locker's on the iced planet of Hoth, if you're late for class tomorrow, you get an F!"

TOP TEN BEST EXCUSES TO GET OUT OF GYM CLASS

 Instead of class, can I wash your car?

 Sorry, but I've been traded to another school.

 I have a sprained eyebrow.

 Have you spoken to my manager about this?

 I already took gym in summer school.

6. Sorry—my brother really needs my kidney.

 7. If my muscles get bigger, I won't fit into my gym suit.

 8. My wage demands exceed your salary cap.

 9. Sorry, I've been diagnosed with Foosball Finger.

 10. I'm allergic to sweat.

PROFILE: WEASEL

WHAT: A small furry animal

COLOR: Brown

ORIGIN: Nobody knows

TAIL: Long

OBSESSION OF: Gordy

RESIDES IN: Lockers, janitor's closet, boiler room, auditorium, cafeteria, bathrooms, classrooms, hallways, gym suits, and backpacks of Polk Middle School

DIET: Garbage, math homework

HIGHEST ELECTED OFFICE: Seventh-grade president

PLACE HE HOPES NEVER TO VISIT: International Weasel Preserve in Paraguay

WHAT HE'D SAY IF HE COULD TALK: "That toilet water really hit the spot!"

TOP TEN PERKS OF BEING THE SCHOOL WEASEL

 Can drink from faculty toilet.

 If you chew Gordy's cleaning supplies, he'll never notice.

 "Weasel" not half as bad a name as "Coconut Head."

 Can wear fur coat to class.

5. Light homework: only chews one to two books per week.

 6. Your friends are a bunch of animals.

 7. Getting to gnaw new people.

 8. President of the Carnivore Club.

 9. Flirting with the vice principal's toupee.

 10. Secure spot under cafeteria "cool" table.

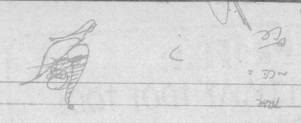

PROFILE:
TIMMY TOOT TOOT

DESCRIPTION: School farter

ACTIVITIES: Blasting the pants cannon, releasing the prisoners

CRIME: Nostril torture

WEAPON OF CHOICE: His farts

PERSONALITY: Silent but deadly

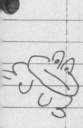

ATTIRE: Belt with cans of pine air freshener

SECRET TO SUCCESS: All baked beans diet

PHILOSOPHY: "Whoever smelt it . . ."

ONLY FRIEND: Lisa Zemo (has permanent stuffed nose)

QUOTE: "Toot toot!"

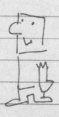

TOP TEN EUPHEMISMS FOR FARTING

 1. Cutting the cheese.

2. Sending a one-gun salute.

3. Sounding the trumpet.

4. Floating an air biscuit.

5. Singeing the carpet.

6. Blowing the horn.

7. Busting a panty burp.

8. Baking brownies.

9. Dropping a bomb.

10. Letting each little bean be heard.

PROFILE: HUGE CREW

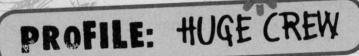

WHAT: Trio of female bullies

OBSESSION: Ned Bigby

ATTIRE: Denim jackets, black T-shirts

APPEARANCE: Livin' large

FINEST MOMENT: Making the Spelling Bees run like scared chickens

FAVORITE QUESTION: "You and what army?"

LEADER: Doris Trembly

SCARIEST MAKEOVER REQUEST: "Want us to rearrange your face?"

REQUIREMENT FOR ADMISSION: Love being tough, love talking about Ned

STUDENT GOVERNMENT: Nominated Ned for class president

QUOTE: "TELL US MORE ABOUT NED! Does he like to swim?"

TOP TEN QUESTIONS ON HUGE CREW APPLICATION

1. When it comes to peanut butter, does Ned prefer smooth or chunky?

 2. What are Ned's favorite animals?

 3. Which word better describes you: *scary* or *frightening*?

 4. Do you take an Xtra-large T-shirt? That's the only kind we have.

 5. Can you work lunch period and homeroom?

6. Do you have references from other kids you've intimidated?

 7. Describe the size and location of your Ned tattoos.

 8. How would you rate your wedgie technique? Are you familiar with the "three-fingered hold"?

 9. Tell us about your work with the organization Ned for Emperor.

 10. Have you ever crushed a guy?

PROFILE: MR. MONROE

JOB: Life science teacher

EXTRACURRICULAR: Sewing club leader, basketball coach

ALIAS: DJ Monroe-o-bot

HIS HIGHEST PRAISE: "There goes the school's best cross-stitcher!"

MOTTO: "Bears happen."

CUTEST LEARNING TOOL: Life Science Baby

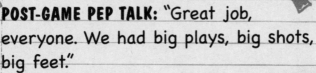

POST-GAME PEP TALK: "Great job, everyone. We had big plays, big shots, big feet."

LAST SEEN: Doing "The Robot" at Dances With Wolves

BEST GUEST LECTURER: Mat Hoffman, greatest BMX rider in vert ramp history

BEST LESSON: Extreme Baby Vert Safety Tips

QUOTE: "What's that, Mr. Powers? You think Monroe don't know b-ball? Yo, gimme the rock!"

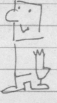

MR. GROSS'S TOP TEN GROOMING TIPS

 Make sure your jacket matches your nose and ear hair.

 Apply deodorant *over* your shirt.

 Please the ladies with "Eau de Tube Socks" aftershave.

 Sweat is nature's hair gel. Sculpt your locks and you'll get the stares— I promise.

 A tie completes an outfit. Remember what you had for lunch by licking it.

6. Always buy pants with flies in them.

 7. Wearing the same clothes every day cuts down on laundry (and friends).

 8. Cut your fingernails in case you have to shake hands. Actually, most people just wave to me!

 9. Keep your breath sweet with chewing gum. I prefer onion-flavored.

 10. Back hair should be neatly coiffed. Use styling mousse.

PROFILE:
CLAIRE SAWYER

OCCUPATION: Future lawyer

REPRESENTS: Half the seventh grade in bully problems, project partner divorces, locker exchanges

CITES: "Page 103, Subsection B, paragraph three..."

ATTIRE: Business suit

CARRIES: Standard boilerplate bully-breaking contract

PERSONALITY: Smart, piranha-like

THREAT: "I'm gonna sue the backpack off that boy."

SIGN-OFF: "Get back to us in study hall with questions and/or conflicts. Bring legal representation."

QUOTE: "You must agree not to wear your underwear outside your clothes. Ever."

TOP TEN SIGNS YOU ARE CLAIRE SAWYER, FUTURE LAWYER

 Your business card says: "Practicing Law Since Sixth Grade."

 Love showing people your legal briefs.

 Cell phone number is 1-800-LETS-SUE.

 You cite legal case of People vs. Coconut Head.

Wear a pinstripe suit to gym.

 You end dates by saying, "No further questions."

 Instead of friends, you have clients.

 Your locker has a receptionist.

 When your friend is given ten days of detention, you get her out in five.

 Fave magazine: *Preteen Attorney*.

PROFILE: LIFE SCIENCE BABY

★ ★ ★

WHAT: Doll

MATERIAL: Plastic

HOME: Life science class

ATTIRE: None

STARE: Vacant

BEHAVIOR: Stiff

LIFE PURPOSE: Help students learn about diaper rash

ACTIVITIES: Getting washed and powdered

GREATEST HONOR: Riding Mat Hoffman's handlebars while he does 360s

WHAT IT WOULD SAY IF IT COULD TALK: "EEEEEEEEEEEEEEK!"

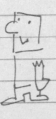

TOP TEN THINGS YOU DON'T WANT TO HEAR IN THE SCHOOL CAFETERIA

 "You don't need a menu. Just look at Mr. Gross's shirt."

 "Has anyone seen the missing lab mice?"

 "I'm not sure how old the Sloppy Joes are. I've only worked here a month."

 "If you find a retainer in there, it's mine."

 "Hey, Lucy, someone finally chose the creamed beets!"

"It's *probably* apple cider."

 "Sorry, no one's allowed in without a haz-mat suit."

 "I'll let the night guy get that."

 "One weasel burger, medium rare."

 "Sorry, the cool table has moved. What did you say your name was?"

PROFILE: SETH POWERS

DESCRIPTION: Basketball star, hottie

WHAT HE IS: Tall

WHAT HE ISN'T: Deep

OBSESSION: Basketball

ATTIRE: Warm-up suit and spinning ball

APPEARANCE: Easy on the eyes

HOME: The gym, cafeteria "cool" table

SKILLS: Spinning basketball on fingertips, looking hot, rhyming

HISTORY PROJECT: Ancient Egyptian basketball

SCREENSAVER: Bouncing basketballs

QUOTE: "My mom told me I had to do something besides basketball or she'd take away my basketball."

NED'S TOP TEN SIGNS YOU WON'T BE SITTING AT THE COOL TABLE

 1. Your best friend is the one you built in Chopsaw's class.

 2. Your date for the dance? The Life Science Baby.

 3. In gym, you practice tae kwon dork.

 4. Claire Sawyer is suing you for geekiness.

 5. The weasel gets more IMs than you do.

6. Not only is Sweeney your project partner, you had to pay him five dollars.

 7. The Spelling Bees look at you and spell U-N-P-O-P-U-L-A-R.

 8. Mr. Wright thinks you're "phat."

 9. Bully Loomer doesn't bother to beat you up.

 10. For a school photo, you "took the wolf." Mom wants copies.

I'M A NED HEAD
I'M A NED HEAD
I'M A NED HEAD
I'M A NED HEAD

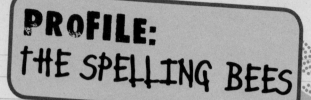

PROFILE:
THE SPELLING BEES

WHAT: A vicious gang of spellers

MEMBERS: King Bee, Queen Bee, and Stinger

WHAT THEY DO: Spell as fast as humanly possible

OBSESSION: Winning the spelling bee

REPUTATION: Most hated bullies at Polk

ATTIRE: Supercool jackets

WEAPON OF CHOICE: Spelling at others

HAUNTING QUESTION: "How many c's in *floccinaucinihilipilification?*"

PET PEEVES: Easy words like *corn, toy,* and *dog*

QUOTE: "Change our math grade or you're going D-O-W-N."

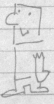

TOP TEN NUMBERS ON NED'S FANTASY SPEED DIAL

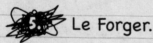 Dial-a-S'more.

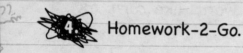 Shaquille O'Neal's cell phone.

 1-800-SNO-CONE.

 Homework-2-Go.

 Le Forger.

 Weasel "B" Gone.

 Agents Cook and Mosely.

8. Cafeteria "cool" table.

 9. Fart Victims Hotline.

 10. Suzie Crabgrass's locker.

PROFILE: BACKPACK BOY

DESCRIPTION: Backpack, with boy attached

REPUTATION: Storage freak

CLAIM TO FAME: Backpack the size of a mini refrigerator

RUMORED TO CONTAIN: Furniture, bicycles, wild animals

SKILLS: Can produce any item in two seconds

SECRET IDENTITY: Superhero

GREATEST PRIDE: Locker leading to backpack showroom

FAVORITES: The Gummy Pack, the Disco Pack

FORMAL ATTIRE: The Evening Pack (all-black)

WHAT HE'S WORKING UP TO: The Behemoth—"double-wide, and custom made by a ninety-two-year-old specialist in Switzerland"

QUOTE: "All I want is a backpack that can microwave a quesadilla. Is that too much to ask?"

TOP TEN CLUES BACKPACK BOY REALLY IS A SUPERHERO

 1. Sometimes wears same clothes.

 2. Powers include X-ray hearing, nose running, and speed reading.

 3. Overheard saying, "To the Backpackmobile!"

 4. Sidekick to Backpack Man.

 5. Already has evil supervillain (Sweeney).

 6. When asked his age, says, "In Earth years?"

 7. Ability to infiltrate foreign environments, like Gordy's office.

 8. Can talk to weasels.

 9. Will reveal secret identity for box of macaroons (oops—that's Le Forger).

 10. Wears refrigerator magnets for fun.

PROFILE: LISA ZEMO

WHO: New student

ACTIVITIES: Sniffling, sneezing, wheezing

BEST FRIEND: Nasal spray

ALLERGIES: Dogs, cats, trees, nuts, wool, and rap videos that exploit women

REPUTATION: A human pharmacy

ADVANTAGE: Can't smell Timmy Toot Toot

CRUSH: Cookie

FINEST MOMENT: Lending Cookie ear and eyedrops to fool Nurse Honsucker and preserve his perfect attendance record

PHILOSOPHY: "Take time to stop and smell the roses. Bring nasal spray."

QUOTE: "We have so much in common. Like how we blew our noses at the same time! Isn't that funny?"

TOP TEN WORST JOKES GOING AROUND POLK MIDDLE SCHOOL

 What kind of book did Timmy Toot Toot write?
A best smeller.

 Why did Suzie Crabgrass bring her dad's charge card to class?
She wanted extra credit.

 Why did Cookie bring his computer to Nurse Honsucker?
It had a virus.

 What do weasels have that no other animal has?
Baby weasels.

 When Vice Principal Crubb found out about Le Forger he brought him into his office.

"Well," said the vice principal, "you'd better have a good excuse for me."
"I do," said Le Forger. "But it'll cost you."

 Did you hear Seth Powers won a gold medal at the Olympics?
He was so proud, he had it bronzed.

 Mr. Wright: Why did you copy Moze's test?
Bitsy: What gave me away?
Mr. Wright: Her name on your paper.

 Why does Gordy mop the floor after a basketball game?
Because the players throw up.

 Ned: I spent seven hours over my science book last night.
Moze: Why?
Ned: It fell under my bed.

 What were the best three years of Bully Loomer's life?
Fifth grade.

NED BIGBY'S TOP TEN REJECTED THEMES FOR THE SCHOOL DANCE

 1. Evening in the Gym.

 2. Enchantment Under the Basketball Net.

 3. Fire Drill!

 4. Leftover Balloons from Spirit Day.

 5. Our Friend the Flatworm.

 6. Suzie Crabgrass Still Won't Dance with You.

1,001 Sweaty Palms.

 See Your Math Teacher Break-
Dance.

 More Rejection, But with Music.

 Salute to the Metric System.

PROFILE:
BILLY "BULLY" LOOMER

OCCUPATION: Bully

COHORTS: Crony, Buzz

LOCKER DECOR: Heavy metal bands and skull stickers

PET PEEVES: Computer geeks, paying for lunch

FAVORITE WRITER: Le Forger

HOBBIES: Writing love poems/beating people up

EXPLANATION: "I'm a complex individual."

SPECIALTIES: Wedgies, ketchup-filled water balloons, cracking open walnuts with his head

WEAPON OF CHOICE: His forehead

LAST BOOK READ: *How to Write Sappy Love Notes in Calligraphy*

QUOTE: "Morning, losers."

CRUSH: Jennifer Mosely

BULLY LOOMER'S TOP TEN ETIQUETTE TIPS

 1. Say "please" when demanding someone's lunch money.

 2. Crush soda cans on forehead to reduce litter.

 3. Be generous—share heavy metal music with everyone on the bus.

 4. When giving wet willies, don't skimp on saliva.

 5. Allow female bullies to cut lunch line ahead of you.

6. No need for long speeches. Stick to "My fists. Your face."

 7. When forcing someone to do your homework, offer to provide a pen.

 8. Neat handwriting makes cheat sheets legible to punks in the back row.

 9. Before smashing two guys' heads together, introduce them.

 10. Don't make people wait. If you promise to beat someone up Friday at 3:30, be on time.

PROFILE: MR. KWEST

OCCUPATION: Computer lab dude

LOVES: *Dungeons & Dragons*

ATTIRE: Geek casual

TEACHING INNOVATION: "The Un-sign-up List"

SOLUTION TO CYBER-CRISIS: "I'll just rewire the fire wire, and uh . . . reboot the boot."

SHORTCOMING: Knows nothing about computers

SECRET FEAR: He'll lose his job (his mom just started charging him rent).

DREADED QUESTION: "Would you like fries with that?"

QUOTE: "Take your butt into the hall. I banish you for seven solar cycles."

WHAT IT MEANS: Don't come back for a week.

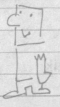

TOP TEN POETIC YEARBOOK SIGNINGS

 1. I won't get sad/I won't get soppy
I'll miss having/Your test to copy
—Bitsy to Moze

2. Roses are red,
Basketballs are orange...
Sorry, that's as far as I got.
—Seth Powers to Suzie

3. If only I were good at art
I'd use this space
To draw a fart
—Timmy Toot Toot to Ned

 4. All year I've tried
To make friends with a girl
If I kiss one more teddy bear
I'm gonna hurl
—Moze to Suzie Crabgrass

 5. Roses are red
Violets are blue
If you fall off your bike
Call 800-LETS-SUE.
—Claire Sawyer to everyone

6. A beagle, a poodle,
A lab, or a mutt,
On the last day of school,
I'm kickin' your butt.

  —Bully Loomer to Ned

7. Noses are red
Summers are hot
The stuff in my nose looks like slime
But it's *not*.

  —Lisa Zemo to Cookie

8. Even tho
I don't h8 u
It doesn't mean
I want 2 d8 u.

  —Cookie to Lisa Zemo

9. 2 Huge
2 B
4-Gotten

  —Doris Trembly to Ned

10. I otter cry
I otter laugh
I otter sign
My otter-graph.

  —School weasel to Gordy

PROFILE: MARTIN QWERLY

ALIAS: Le Forger

REPUTATION: School's best note forger

SKILLS: Will forge note for any student in exchange for a box of macaroons

WHAT TWENTY BOXES BUY: His pager number

OWNS: 328 educational computer games

DREAM DATE: Big-screen movie about dust

SCARIEST PROMISE: "For this talent show, I'm going to perform something more 'street.'"

ELECTION SLOGAN: "Vote Early. Vote Qwerly."

PHYSICAL BOAST: "I'm only eight inches and fifty-five pounds away from maximum butt-kicking ability."

QUOTE: "Let's tell secrets! I didn't change my underwear this morning. . . ."

TOP TEN QUESTIONS THAT KEEP NED UP AT NIGHT

 1. Is the cafeteria cool table really cooler?

 2. A thousand-word report?! Do I *know* a thousand words?

 3. What if the Huge Crew has branches in other cities?

 4. What's in mystery chow mein?

5. How do I learn 200 years of American history by fourth period?

 6. What if Bully Loomer didn't know I was kidding?

 7. What if Moze isn't pretending to like beany-kitties?

 8. Is tether-weasel a sport?

 9. What if Cookie really is a cyborg?

 10. When will Suzie realize I'm the hottest guy in school?

PROFILE: MR. SWEENEY

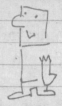

JOB: Teacher, mad scientist

LAUGH: Maniacal

CLASSIFICATION: Evil-teacher-whose-goal-is-to-destroy-you

CRUELEST INVENTION: The science-puzzler word game

CRUELEST ACT: Holding class hostage on Pizza Day

NED'S PLEA: "Let them go, Sweeney. They're hungry. They smell melted cheese."

CHILDHOOD PET: Algae

CRUELEST ASSIGNMENT: 10,000-word report on chlorophyll

MOZE ON SWEENEY: "Either he's lost his mind or that's a really fun chair."

QUOTE: "Mr. Bigby. Looking forward to seeing you today! Mwa-ha-ha-ha!"

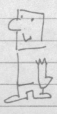

TOP TEN LOCKER STICKERS

 1. I Brake for Weasels.

 2. Honk if You Love Suzie Crabgrass.

 3. Keep On Farting.

 4. Help! I've Been Huge-Crewed!

 5. I Took the Wolf.

 6. Kiss me, I'm Coconut Head!

 7. GO, POLK WOLVES!

8. Have You Hugged Your Life Science Baby Today?

 9. I survived the Atomic Flush.

 10. Honk if You *Are* Suzie Crabgrass.

TOP TEN OTHER USES FOR THIS BOOK

 Two words: paper airplanes.

 Re-cover it with the jacket of *Advanced Astrophysics*.

 Juggle a few copies at a talent show.

 Use it to cover your face on photo day.

 Wear it under your shirt to ward off death rays.

6. Stick it in backpack next to inflatable raft.

 7. One book = 41 origami birds.

 8. Handy coaster for iced drinks.

 9. Use as place-saver at "cool" table.

 10. Emergency toilet paper.

The end